ECSTACY

ECSTACY

GEETHA MOHAN

Translated by
SEEMA PRADEEP

GULF BOOK
SERVICES

Published by **Gulf Book Services Ltd**

20-22 Wenlock Road, London,
NI 7GU, UK
Email: info@gulfbooks.co.uk

GULF BOOK Office No: G23,
SERVICES Sharjah Publishing City Free Zone
Sharjah – UAE

First Published by Gulf Book Services Ltd

ISBN: 978-1-917529-30-3
Year: October 2025

Typeset in Merriweather by Madhavi. S

Introduction

Words That Carry Truth – Unclad, Undraped

In today's world, one of the most powerful acts is a woman writing her heart out. Whether it is through her life experiences, a novel, a piece of prose or poetry, an academic thesis, a journal, or any form of expression—it carries immense social significance.

For a woman, expressing her emotions, reasoning, and opinions is not an easy task. Regardless of the genre she belongs to, society often expects her to prioritize her family above all else. But for a man, these expectations are different. That is how the society demands differently from a man and a woman she is stuck between her limitations.

This is the societal imbalance that women face—caught in a web of restrictions. Husbands and sons often grant only "necessary" freedoms, and women, in turn, sometimes accept this as what they deserve. There are still women who believe that male dominance at home is normal, even noble—sacrificing their preferences for a society that has conditioned them to see it as fate.

But from such a stifling space, women have slowly risen. It is only in recent years that strong and independent women have emerged—resilient, like warriors surviving a battlefield of internal and external struggles. This transformation didn't happen overnight; it came after generations of silent battles, fought within.

From this evolving world, authors like **Geetha Mohan** have emerged—women who dare to use words as their medium for truth. Her book *"Matthu"* must be read within this context.

Today, new-generation women are navigating multiple roles—emotionally, rationally, and socially. They're achieving prominence across fields, while maintaining a delicate balance between tradition and modernity. Writers like Geetha Mohan reflect this balance in their work.

In a world full of modern ideas, even those women who claim independence may hesitate to express themselves fully. Not due to a lack of talent, but often out of concern that their voices might redirect attention away from their traditional familial roles.

A writer cannot journey through the world of literature without an understanding of both the ancient and the modern. Geetha Mohan embodies this balance. Her stories explore themes like love, lust, friendship, family, relationships, and brotherhood—rich in both cultural context and emotional depth.

"*Matthu*" (*Ecstasy*), for instance, is one such story that centers around a pair of intoxicating eyes—and the dream they awaken. But this dream is not of a king in shining armor. Instead, it is of a beggar who gazes at her with love, wonder, and unfiltered awe.

This story delves into love and lust in their rawest, most honest forms. It portrays how deeply a woman can yearn for physical satisfaction—not as something shameful, but as a natural and essential part of her being. Geetha Mohan boldly asserts that such emotions are not to be hidden or silenced, but to be embraced, understood, and experienced.

While society often frowns upon women who openly express such desires, the author dismantles this taboo. She reveals that these feelings are not myths or vulgarities—they are naked truths of womanhood. These truths deserve to be acknowledged, not judged.

Science has long affirmed the importance of emotional and physical intimacy in human well-being, and this story reflects that truth through poetic simplicity. Her lust, in this narrative, doesn't overpower her—it becomes part of her. It flows through her dreams, where she dares to explore what reality often denies her.

Written in accessible, straightforward language, *Matthu* is a beautifully expressed exploration of the inner world of a woman—raw, real, and resonant.

Several stories in *Matthu* explore love and lust beyond a woman's teenage years—an age often overlooked by most writers. When such themes are addressed, they tend to stir controversy. Society still finds it difficult to accept that older women, too, can experience deep longing, passion, and desire. As a result, these stories are often dismissed—not because they lack literary value, but because they dare to express what many consider taboo.

But isn't that the law of nature? Human emotions don't fade with age. Love, lust, and the need for connection continue throughout life. Geetha Mohan challenges this societal silence in her stories, and that's exactly what moved me most about her work. She gives voice to emotions that have long been suppressed or ignored, especially in women beyond their so-called "prime."

A writer should have the freedom to think beyond the boxes society creates—to write beyond the columns designed by someone else. And that's what Geetha has done.

Stories like *"Nottam"* (*The Look*) delicately release emotions like bubbles, bursting gently through simple, poetic lines. Geetha Mohan has a rare ability to convey deep feelings with minimal words, letting her readers experience emotion in its purest, most unfiltered form.

Another striking story, *"Aavesham"* (*The Impulse*), is particularly haunting. It begins with a man sitting alone on a beach, where he notices a woman seemingly ready to end her life. What draws him to her isn't her sorrow, but the raw beauty of her body—the innocence still etched into her flesh. Driven by impulse, he feels no guilt in seeking physical pleasure, thinking perhaps it would offer her some final comfort, some fleeting fulfillment before she disappears forever.

But after their union, when he asks why she wanted to die, her answer pierces through his assumptions. She reveals that she is suffering from Aids—a revelation that fills him with shame, guilt, and a sickening awareness of how wrong his intentions were. Geetha doesn't tell us what happens next. She ends the story there—abrupt, unresolved, and devastating.

That is the brilliance of her storytelling. She doesn't decorate her endings with dramatic conclusions or moral commentary. Instead, she allows her characters to drift beyond he page, leaving readers with the emotional weight of their choices. She trusts us to sit with the discomfort, to reflect, and to seek our own meanings.

"Vayassariyikkal" (Puberty) is yet another powerful story that captures the evolving journey of a woman—her transformation not just at the onset of menstruation, but also during the often-ignored phase of menopause. Geetha Mohan emphasizes that a woman's body and emotions continue to shift across different stages of life, and each transition carries its own silent weight.

One of the most remarkable aspects of Geetha's writing is her ability to distill deep emotions into simple, powerful lines. She uses only a handful of characters, yet she manages to evoke the most intimate and essential aspects of a woman's experience. Her stories don't sprawl—they are brief, concentrated, and quietly piercing.

Except for "Thalappaavu" (The Sacred Headgear), most of the stories in this collection center around women. Rather than telling full life stories, Geetha captures moments— snapshots of feeling and transformation. Each story is like a small offering, placed in a nutshell, gently in front of us, to read with ease.

There is another compelling story in *Matthu*, centered around a woman's fear and emotional turmoil. She plans to visit a temple with her guest, but her husband unexpectedly arrives home. She has a silent friend—her lover—who remains unaware of this sudden change, as she doesn't get a chance to inform him. The next morning, she must accompany both her husband and the guest to the temple. Before entering, she is asked to hand over her phone to her husband, who knows her lock code. Her phone contains intimate, undeleted messages from her lover.

As she rushes through the temple rituals, her prayers are not for peace or prosperity, but for one desperate wish—that her husband doesn't read those messages. Her heart races with fear and shame. But as she exits the temple, she finds him calmly talking to a relative, someone coincidentally named after the lord. She feels a wave of relief wash over her, realizing he hasn't seen the messages. As she holds his hand, a strange sense of security returns to her—a moment of silent reconciliation between her fear and her reality.

This story, like many in the collection, reflects the intricate emotional world of women. What's remarkable is that even when portraying a man's thoughts or role, it's always through the lens of a woman's experience. The stories in *Matthu* don't present these emotional or physical challenges as problems—they are the realities of life, laid bare with honesty and grace. That's what makes the book so unique.

There are also stories that give voice to the pain of abandoned elderly women and the loneliness they endure. It serves as a realization, a quiet awakening for the new generation of readers.

Another remarkable aspect of Geetha's writing is her unique storytelling style. There are no long introductions, no elaborate backstories, and no conventional build-ups. Her stories begin right at the heart of the moment—plunging directly into the core emotion or situation. She doesn't introduce the characters or lay out morals for the reader to follow. There are no decorative frills. Just the truth—raw, undraped, and honest.

This simplicity is what makes her stories short, crisp, and powerful. Every word feels essential, and every line carries weight. For me, this stripped-down form of writing was one of the most compelling aspects of the book. It felt as though the stories weren't dressed up for effect—they were bare, real, and deeply human.

The collection contains twenty-two stories, including one titled *"Patti"* (*The Dog*). Each of them, in its own way, traces the emotional and mental journey of a woman—through different phases of life, different struggles, and different forms of strength.

The renowned writer Leelavathy Teacher, whom we all take immense pride in, once wrote about the legendary poet Balamani Amma:

"The energy needed for the revolutionary thinking that persists behind deconstructive narratives cannot arise from anything other than the sharpness of intellect, the tenderness of heart, the unwavering sense of righteousness, and a soul that flows with compassion."

This profound statement does not apply to Balamani Amma alone, but to all writers who have made a meaningful impact on society through the art of their writing. I have deeply felt the truth of these words.

A woman is created with, and for, a powerful purpose—as reflected in Leelavathy Teacher's words. And *Matthu* by Geetha Mohan stands as a true testament to that purpose. It is not just a collection of stories, but a declaration of a woman's voice, strength, vulnerability, and truth.

Once a student once asked Prophet Muhammad (Nabi):
"Who should I respect the most?"
"Your mother," he replied.
"Then who?"
"Your mother."
"And after that?"
"Again, your mother."
Only then does the father take the fourth place.

This is the value of a mother—a woman—in the home, in society, and in every individual's life.

And yet, many women—and some of the men in their lives—live without fully realizing this truth and power. We must encourage and recognize every small act, every silent strength a woman shows. Among these, the most powerful is a woman's ability to write—and to write about women.

Half of the world of literature belongs to women. It is born from them, inspired by them, and sustained by their voices. And in that half, **Geetha Mohan has carved her space—with her quiet, fearless words and her delicate yet unshakable lines.**

(Translated from the Malayalam version originally written by Thanuja S Bhattathiri)

Foreward

Have you seen the blue litmus paper turn red?

Istanbul is the cultural and economic center of Turkey. Historically, it was initially known as Byzantium and later as Constantinople.

Before Christ, around 660 BC, King Byzas of the Greeks established the city of Byzantium on the banks of Bosporus. This marks the beginning of Istanbul's history. Byzantium, often embroiled in conflicts between the Greek and Persian empires, was a city that frequently changed hands. Roman Emperor Constantine the Great, renamed the city Constantinople, making it the capital of the Roman Empire. Constantine, the first Roman emperor to convert to Christianity, played a pivotal role in the spread of Christianity through the establishment of Constantinople.

In 1453, Ottoman Sultan Mehmed II captured Constantinople, bringing an end to the Byzantine Empire. Under Ottoman rule, for long 470 years, the city flourished as a center of Islamic culture and power. The name Constantinople was gradually replaced with Istanbul, a name that resonated with the Turkish-speaking populace. The name 'Constantinople' was difficult for the Turks to pronounce, and hence it was named Istanbul. That's what the enemies mocked.

In Orhan Pamuk's novel '*My Name is Red*', one can see Istanbul's evolution. The city, which has oscillated between Christianity and Islam, has been a melting pot of diverse cultures. Like many other countries, there were people and periods when certain communities faced persecution. I am now talking about one such person.

In 1806, the British attacked Constantinople. The general then was Sébastini whose war tricks defeated the English. The Sultan of Istanbul at that time was Selim. "What must I give you in return? I can cover you with anything that you want". The sultan asked Sebastini and took him to his chambers. For the first time, a general was allowed into the Sultan's private quarters. Sébastini observed the sultan's wives closely, one by one. The Sultan, without hesitation, asked, "Do you find any of these women attractive?" Without hesitation Sebastiani pointed his fingers to one of them on whom his eyes were glued to. "I will send her to you" the Sultan promised and bid farewell to Sebastini. He waited until late night for Sultan's gift but what came instead was the woman's head on a plate, along with a note from the Sultan himself.

'Beloved general, being a Muslim, I cannot offer anything to someone from my community to anyone who is a Christian. However, through this, you can be assured that this woman will not be anyone else's.'"

Capturing a piece of the body that has been plucked from the source and delicately placing it on the platter is what a preface is all about. Lying so in the initial pages, it calls out, 'Dear writer, I am certain through this that these lines of yours that I love, belong to you and no one else.'"

The dazzling theatrics that make a sudden entrance at the most unexpected moment, meant to captivate, but to repeat lines already read and left ungrasped would only test the reader's patience, that is what a narrator does. This book doesn't need someone who enters the story dragging a trail of melodrama.

So let me say this—I will not pick up all the good words and platter it here.

Geetha Mohan, for me, is Istanbul, not Constantinople. There's nothing complicated in her, none in her writing, and none in her being. Gardev had written, "Do not approach art with your emotions". But Geetha Mohan, the storyteller, stands opposed to that. She approaches art with the whole of her emotions. Her narratives wander through every shade of the people she intimately knows, in all their unfiltered intensity. The care and the conflict the storyteller feels towards those around her are all present in these stories. Geetha Mohan's storytelling makes the reader pause and wonder — 'Is this me?'

In one of the stories, there's a woman who enters the temple holding her heart out, fearing if her husband Venuveten might read the fragmented messages of her lover. Suma knows that her world would collapse if he sees that. If prayer holds any power, then God must step outside and sit beside him, distracting him with stories so that he doesn't even bother to look at her phone. Is there such a god? I won't say whether there is or isn't. That answer lies in the story "*Eeshvaro Rakshatu*"

Yes, there are moments when we feel, this must be God. Often, it's that very feeling, that illusion, that performs the magic within a story. But in these stories, everything is real. The people in them are real. And that is why their silences, their agony, carry such depth and weight in each story.

To the question, 'Why was this world created?', Ramana Maharshi once gave an answer. Creation is not for good, nor for evil. It simply is, just as it should be. According to him, it is the human mind that knits all the webs with meaning around it. It is only through that web we perceive the world. And we interpret everything solely according to what interests us.

For instance, a woman is not just a woman. For one, she may appear as a mother. But to another, she might be a lover. And yet in that lover's eyes, someone else might see a sister. In this way, the same woman is perceived in many forms. Interestingly, it is often these very men, who love women differently in different forms, claim to fear snakes. The same person can love some living beings and feel a deep-rooted aversion toward others. The man who gazes longingly at a woman might neither see the grass nor a stone with the same feeling. If he did, they wouldn't be ignored. The truth is, this question of what holds value and what doesn't is the root cause of all suffering in the world.

Creation is like a banyan tree. Birds come to eat its fruit. They rest peacefully on its branches. People find shade under it and enjoy its freshness. But for some, it is a death tree, they hang themselves down it to end their lives.

The problem lies not in the tree, not in the world, but in the mind of man.

There stands a tree with branches wide enough to offer both rest and stillness. How we use it — that is our choice. Birds and other creatures never seem to misuse it the way humans do. God is not partial, not the kind to give comfort to one and sorrow to another. In his creation, everything has its place. It is we who keep making choices. And the pain of creation lies exactly here, only humans make choices that make them attached to goodness, to health, to beauty.

What runs through all of Geetha Mohan's stories is the pain, Ramana Maharshi spoke of. In the story "Thirumurivu", there's a writer who, despite having paper and pen right beside her, cannot write even a single letter.

But when she begins to write about love, words flow unfiltered, and there is no writer's block at all

Geetha Mohan doesn't just show this in one story, but across her work, she proves that love is like a concentrated, corrosive capsule. This trembling truth pulses through every story, some more and some less. The protagonist has no doubt on which balm is needed to soothe a bruised ankle. But it is Ammuchechi, in one story, who quietly drags us through the magic of that very balm, only to stroke the wound and ease the pain in no time.

I once wrote in an old love letter, 'Love is like hydrochloric acid — powerful.

I still feel that way. I always used to like acids. You must be wondering! "Will it not burn?" You're right. It is true."

Have you ever seen blue litmus paper turn red? That was the first magic I ever witnessed in life. That's where my fear of burning began and that's also where my fascination with acids took root.

In all the stories I've read since, what I've searched for is that same magic — the magic of blue litmus turning red. The art of transformation. The sting of acid rain that arrives just in time to corrode me.

There are two types of acids — mild and concentrated. When concentrated nitric acid and hydrochloric acid are mixed, the resulting solution is known in chemistry as *aqua regia*. In literature, it is called ,*Royal water or the Kings water.*"

"In the 13th century, the European alchemist known as Pseudo-Geber wrote of *aqua regia* in his texts — a miraculous liquid that could dissolve gold.

The world dismissed it, mocking it as alchemists' madness. Yet, in 1940, science quietly confirmed that *aqua regia* could, indeed, dissolve even the noblest of metals, that too when they realised it would impact them

It was during the Second World War, around 1940, at Niels Bohr's institute in Copenhagen, the capital of Denmark, the incident happened. German troops were intruding in, any moment, the Nazis could break through the door.

Inside a hidden locker at the institute lay two Nobel gold medals, secretly stored — those of Max von Laue and James Franck. "Should we bury them now?" Bohr's colleague, Hevesy, asked, even though he knew that it would be dug out. Bohr stood frozen, helpless.

Then came the idea — not from Bohr, but from Hevesy himself. 'This is my last idea,' Hevesy said, 'don't stop me.'

When Bohr heard the word *aqua regia*, he rose and walked away without another word. A man who knew science should not even think of such baseless things. However

Hevesy was already holding the beaker that had the medals in it. Dissolved. That was his reply.

Since that day, *aqua regia* is indeed the Royal water.

"There are people like aqua regia — rare, unmatched, and capable of dissolving even those who thought they were indissoluble. They are made from the fusion of two powerful acids: nitric acid, which burns, and hydrochloric acid, which holds the heat in silence.

Geetha Mohan, to me, is one such person. From the moment I first knew her, she has been melting me. And now, her stories arrive like scalding visions, doing the same.

"I find myself deeply drawn to the presence of women. I admire their beauty. I am moved by their openness, and equally, by their silences. It was Samuel Johnson who once wrote about women like this.

I feel it is Samuel Johnson who lives mostly in all the husbands and the wives are forced to remain silent.

But Mohanetten is not like the husband in Dr. Johnson's theory. He doesn't seek his wife's silence. He walks the same path she walks, and that image lives vividly in this book.

You will see it in the story about Manju's father, a story where Geetha herself is the protagonist.

The storyteller portrays Mohanettan, Sharjah, and everything around, carefully, with deliberate strokes. In many ways, Geetha Mohan's stories are autobiographical. Her narrative world is rich with glimpses of husbands, lovers, neighbours, and friends, sometimes with real names, sometimes renamed, crossing in and out of identity, echoing and transforming as they go.

Carlyn G. Berk once wrote that women's writings begin with her body. Geetha Mohan is doing just that. It is just her beginning. In her stories, her characters walk adorned, with coloured lips, refusing to offer themselves either to the compelling call of lesbians who beckon them, or to men who are hungry for physical pleasures.

These women remain untouchable — not passive but composed.

And yet, these same women also carry within them the voices of those who once said, *'You were never the one whom I wanted.'* They gather those words, hold them to their hearts like sharp stones, and set fire to them, silently, and, fiercely. That is the kind of women in Geetha Mohan's stories.

She is a lover with delirious dreams, her eyes hold a land that none can capture. You might have read about the unnamed and unclaimed letters that try to capture her soul and existence. But that doesn't destroy her.

This is the truth that she says to the world.

I have an identity. I am Geetha Mohan, an Indian writer living in Sharjah. And I will tell you the story of women who knows how to engulf you in desire and who knows how to transform them into fire if needed.

It is through her characters, that the storyteller speaks to you, saying "Read me.'"

There is love, desire, lust ,yes. But what remains, what endures after all of it, is realisation.

When young girls first begin menstruating, there's a celebration. But we never say *'she menstruated'* and in Malayalam, we say *'Thirandu kalyanam'.* We have memories of the joy once poured into that moment of becoming.

Much later, when fed up with the colours of life, the narrator says *even revulsion is a kind of a moment of becoming.*

"Once, my body bloomed with thirst, now, at forty-five, it ripens with withdrawal. This is enough."

"*The Writer's Quotation Book*" published by Penguin contained a delightful anecdote about the American humorist S.J. Perelman. When his first book was released, Groucho Marx, perhaps the greatest comedian of the television era, wrote:

"Perelman, from the moment I picked up your book to the moment I put it down, I was convulsed with laughter"

I've often thought I must read that book someday.

But today, I find myself saying —

"Dear Geethechi, from the moment I picked up your book to the moment I put it down, I was disturbed. My eyes were filled with sorrow. I was overwhelmed, wordlessly. Someday, I will put aside all my emotions and read it again without any strings attached. And then, I will write its preface. This is all that I can say out of my emotions for now."

(Translated from the Malayalam version originally written by Lijeesh Kumar)

Preface

Geetha Mohan, daughter of Mr. K.P. Krishnan (LIC of India) and Mrs. Lakshmikutty, hails from Payyanur in the Kannur district of Kerala. A graduate in Hindi from Payyanur College, she has been residing in Sharjah for the past thirty years with her husband, Mr. Mohan Kumar, who is associated with the Sharjah Book Authority.

"Matthu", her first book, is a beautifully composed collection of twenty-two short stories. The book stands out not with grandiose language or forced emotions, but with its simplicity and grace. Each story flows gently, touching the soul like soft waves, offering a heartfelt and visually rich literary experience.

Whether exploring love, lust, friendship, or family, the stories in *"Matthu"* are steeped in real life experiences. The characters come alive without formal introductions or elaborate descriptions—they simply emerge within the flow of the story, fully formed and deeply familiar. Each narrative feels like a glimpse through the window of the house next door, so close, so real, and so relatable. These are stories you recognize, emotions you've felt, and moments you've lived.

Personally, I have seen myself, and many women I've known, in the pages of Matthu. The stories resonate with a quiet power, capturing everyday moments with such authenticity that they feel intimately familiar. It's this honest reflection of life that makes the book both moving and readable.

Why a Translation?

This is my first attempt at translating a book, carrying it from its native soil to another. Malayalam is in my roots, and I have always held deep admiration for the language, its authors, and the worlds they create. I know I may never be able to craft even a single piece of literature like theirs.

So all I tried to do, humbly and honestly, is try to present a glimpse of that magic on a new platter, in a language that can carry its soul across borders. This translation is a tribute, an offering, and a quiet celebration of a literary tradition I deeply cherish.

Why Matthu?

When you try a new recipe, you start with the most familiar ingredient. When you attempt a new choreography, you choose the music that moves you the most. When you begin a drawing, you reach for the colour you're most comfortable with.

In the same way, when I decided to explore a new style of writing—where I wasn't just translating words, but carrying the soul of the literature, honouring the author, and staying true to their emotions—I knew I needed a starting point that felt safe and trusted. I needed an author who believed in me enough to hand over their book, their creation, their baby—trusting that I would care for it with the heart of a mother.

Geetha Mohan said yes even before I could finish my request. I call her Chechi, and it holds both my love and respect, but within me, there's a small heart that experiences a mother's love from her. She has a way of making everyone feel seen, valued, and cherished. I don't know how she does it, but everyone who knows her feels special in her presence. That's a kind of magic only a mother can give to all her children, equal, unbiased, and endlessly warm.

Matthu is a book filled with the raw, unpolished truths of everyday life—simple, honest, and deeply human. From the moment I read it, I felt it needed to travel far beyond its original home.

What I have done is a very simple translation—no embellishments, no flourishes—just an honest attempt to carry every emotion, every feeling, every truth, and every heartbeat of these stories into another language.

I only hope I have done justice to it in every way I can, and that its readers will give it a place in their hearts and their homes.

Thank you, Chechi, for letting me attempt it.

Let your Matthu and our Ecstacy travel to heights.

Lovingly yours,

Seema Pradeep

Contents

1
A Woman's Heart

It was a scorching summer. The sun blazed down on the road like a furnace. She finished her prayers and walked out through the west entrance of the temple. The heat was already draining, and the sweet she'd had as temple offering only made her thirstier.

There it was—that small shop. And inside, the handsome man selling cold drinks and snacks. She felt the pull of buttermilk on her parched throat and went straight to the counter.

"Two glasses of buttermilk, please," she said.

His words hung in the air like a soft tune. She blinked, surprised. Then her lips curled into a smile.

She blushed, thanked him sincerely, and gulped the buttermilk, which now felt even cooler with the ice of his compliments. And from such a handsome man! What more could she ask for?

He handed her the second glass, and as she sipped, she could feel a different kind of coolness spreading inside her— flavored not just with spices and salt, but with attention and admiration.

She walked away, feeling a little taller in her perfectly stitched blouse.

Still flushed from the moment, she pulled out her phone and called her tailor.

"Sir! Everyone is praising the blouse and its fitting on me—no words! I'm coming soon with more blouse pieces. Sarees matching to them, I'll get later. Okay, right Sir!"

The cutting master on the other end was delighted. His work had made it into conversation, and more business was on the way. That night, her WhatsApp was flooded with hearts—red, purple, green, and gold—from the tailor himself.

The next morning, she was up early. Blouse pieces, then matching sarees—that was the plan. She wore the same blouse again, proud and pleased. She called Jacob, the auto driver, to pick her up.

Just as she stepped out, her neighbour Renuka dashed in, uninvited as always, curiosity bouncing in her eyes.

"Where are you going so dressed up this early?" she asked, sitting down before being offered a seat.

And then came the questions, one after another—fishing lines thrown out, waiting to hook some gossip.

Finally, cornered, she gave in. "Yesterday, the guy at the temple drink shop, he said something nice about my blouse. It felt good."

Renuka's eyes widened. She sat up straight, as if the story had just begun.

"Him? Oh my god. That guy? He's a total flirt! Last month, he told me the exact same thing—about my blouse! And would you believe, he said it to Bindu, the beautician, too. Don't go by his words. He's a woman-pleaser, that one. He'll sweet-talk anyone who walks in."

A pause settled between them like dust. She blinked, the compliment cooling in her mind now, no longer icy fresh. The magic had melted.

Just then, Jacob arrived, honking once from the street.

She took a breath, grabbed her handbag, and stepped out.

"Where to, Madam?" Jacob asked, cheerfully.

"Let's go meet Vatsala," she said. "She's shifted to that house near the banyan tree, past the main road. She had been sick for a while, and I haven't had the time to meet her"

The blouse pieces could wait. After all the compliments were fake.

Sometimes, a change of plan isn't a delay—it's a detour written by destiny, saving you from falling into foolishness disguised as flattery.

2
Ammuchechi

This vacation was too short—hardly a week in my hometown. And my hometown, my lords, is Krishna's land: Guruvayur.

In that one week, I was hardly left with any time. There are people there who love me like no one else—people who light up my days and nights with their presence. The only pain I carry every time I leave is that I am never able to experience all the love waiting for me. I have to leave some halfway, and some have to wait until my next visit. Yet,

I'm grateful. To be able to return often, to be welcomed with such warmth — it's a blessing not everyone is lucky to have.

And then, there's Ammuchechi.

The moment I land and step inside my home, she comes running and sticks to me like glue. She lives a little far and can barely walk, but she drags her feet just to be beside me—wherever I go. Like a shadow, like a silent protector, she walks with me without even needing a word. No one should talk to me, no one should bother me—and if it's a man, then God save him from her wrath. Sometimes I feel like I should take her back with me. That's how deep her love runs. And if I am alone at home? She won't leave my side for a second.

She was scared for me this time. I had fractured my foot a few weeks ago, though it had mostly healed. I didn't tell her until I reached. When I did, she looked at my feet. They were a little swollen from travel and aching. Her eyes welled up with tears. Without a word, she rushed home and returned with a small bottle.

She made me sit on the sofa, gently lifted my right foot into her lap, and started applying oil to my swollen ankle. Her hands were soft, careful, and warm. It hurt, yes, but there was something soothing in that pain. Something only, she could give.

At some point, I must have dozed off, lulled by her touch, her presence. When I woke up, she was still sitting there, my foot in her lap, her head resting against the wall, fast asleep.

I slowly pulled my foot away, trying not to wake her. And that's when I noticed it — the pain was gone. The swelling, too. Out of curiosity, I picked up the bottle she had used.

It was *just hair oil.*

That moment, life taught me a lesson once again:Love is the best medicine. It can heal pain that no prescription can.

When it was time to leave, I had just one prayer to my Lord"Please, Krishna, let Ammuchechi stay like this—with me, forever.

My Ammuchechi."

3
Awakening-the beginning

With a big desire, to write a story, I took a pen, gathered a few papers and laid it down on the table.

Made sure the pen can write, yes! It does...

Words and phrases came flooding like waves, and I was filled with the greed of writing volumes, but I was lost.

As I sat down, thoughts swirled in my mind like leaves caught in a gust of autumn wind. The blank pages before me were like a canvas waiting to be filled with the colours of imagination. The room was quiet, I closed my eyes, inhaling deeply, and let my mind wander into the realms of possibilities.

What should I write about?

Whom should I write about? Shall I write about "him". Ohh no, he doesn't deserve to be in a book. He doesn't even deserve the place I give to the squeezed-out refill of my pen.

Then what shall I write about! May be my childhood?

But then I realised that this was not what I was gifted with.

To write! Even God did not bless me with the skill of putting my thoughts in a paper.

I really respect all those great writers who easily play with words and throw it on neat lines, to make a book.

A deep sense of sorrow dipped me in sweat, and I felt like I was drowning in an emptiness that filled in my little room.

I switched on the fan that called me from the table, and I swept on to my bed. That was the only solution I always had, when my dreams failed. The cool breeze soothed my forehead like a lullaby, and I dozed off.

"My girl"

He called me, and I woke up from my slumber. He was not my father, but he was something more than that. The room, as he entered, had a divine smell. This was his home, and I had liked it at the first sight. It had been only a few months since I bought this home. Some places give a sense of peace; this was one of those places.

One day, I fell sick, shattered with fever and collapsed. When I opened my eyes, I was in bed with him sitting beside me. Aunty had some hot gruel in her hand with a spicy coconut side dish. I refused, saying it was trouble for them and as she forced me to have it, he asked me, "Who am I?" I replied, "Like my father."

Was he, my father? Or who was he? The man who owned the house before me. But he became a source of energy and solace for me as I had lost my father when I was a child, and I had known little what a father's love was like.

"If you think I am your father, then you are my daughter until I die," he said. I wiped the tears that silently rolled out of my eyes.

The next day, he came with a beautifully wrapped gift box. It was a big one. It was my favourite idol of Lord Krishna. And when it came from the hands that hold the rosary, the statue had more divinity in it. With tears in my eyes, I grasped my Lord and thanked him. He said, "You will from now on remember me, in your prayers."

As he said, a few days later, he passed away, vanishing into a world that was far. I lost another part of me that had all his love and warmth.

Aunty came to my room after two days of his demise, and gave me the table fan and said, "It is uncle's. Let it give you his blessings and make you feel his presence in your loneliest moments." She held me tight and cried all her sorrow out.

I looked at the fan now as I drowned into his thoughts. Its soothing and cool breeze, filled with his love, caressed my eyes that had the wetness of his memories in me.

What else can I write about! Who else can fill my book!

Here was my first story!

About the man who filled the gap that my father had left. A man who brought back my father to me through his love and kindness. A man who once again made me what my father wanted me to be.

I hooked my face to the pillow, wiped off the little smile that blossomed on my lips. Words were happily calling me, ready to be set on the papers that were on the table.

And after all happiness is when thoughts can craft stories that change human lives!

A sense of accomplishment washed over me. The desire to write had blossomed into a tale that would inspire others, just as it had inspired me. And so, with a contented smile, I laid down my pen, knowing that this was just the beginning of many more to come.

(This story is my dedication to the man who sold his mansion to clear his debts , moved to a small home and who is now resting in his six foot grave free from all liabilities)

4
Change of Fate!

The sun had long since dipped behind the coconut palms when Meenakshiyamma stirred in her bed.

"Dear Radha," she called softly, her voice floating out of the dimly lit room. "Have they left? Padhmanaban, Lalitha, and the kids?"

Radha walked in, wiping her hands on her saree. She sat gently beside the older woman, brushing a loose wisp of hair from Meenakshiyamma's forehead.

"Yes, Amma. They left."

Meenakshiyamma's eyes narrowed slightly. "They came to invite us for the wedding, didn't they?"

Radha hesitated. "Yes... They asked about you. They wanted to come in, but... they thought they shouldn't disturb you."

The old woman gave a sad smile, gripping Radha's hand.

"I overheard them. They didn't even mention my name. Not once. They walked past my door to see the terrace plants, laughing... as if I didn't exist. I was right there, Radha. Longing just for a glance. Just a hello." Her voice cracked. "How many years we lived together under the same roof."

Radha's heart ached. She had noticed it too — the way familiarity had turned cold, how the presence of the old woman had faded into the background of everyone else's busy lives.

"I'll go bring your dinner, Amma," she whispered, needing to escape the weight in the room.

Left alone, Meenakshiyamma rose slowly and walked to
the washroom. She leaned toward the mirror, squinting
to see clearly. The face that stared back was etched with
wrinkles, once glowing with the yellow hue of turmeric
her mother used to brighten her youthful skin. Now, it was
tired, folded, faded by time.

Her neck, once smooth and graceful, now looked like thin skin draped over bone. Her hands, once adorned with bangles, were now pale, veined, and dry. She gently applied sacred ash to her forehead and folded her hands in prayer, as she did every night, wishing only for a peaceful end.

As she returned to her bed, her thoughts swirled again with an aching nostalgia.

Tears welled up and slipped down her cheeks. She wiped them quickly with her saree pallu. *When no one sees your tears, they are nothing but salt water*, she thought.

"Amma," Radha's voice brought her back.

Radha came in with a plate of food and placed it gently beside her. Meenakshiyamma began to eat slowly, lost again in the stories of her past.

"You know, Radha. I too had an evergreen time. Sundays used to be full of people coming to see me for marriage. Proposals every week. My mother, even with her headaches from cooking with firewood — was always ready to make tea and snacks for them."

"She would be proud when people praised my looks and character. My father would find faults in every single proposal, no matter how good they were. He would say, *'My Meenakshikutty deserves better!'* And he would smile, showing those beetle-nut-stained teeth of his."

"Eventually, they did find the best partner they could for me... and life moved on. But the clock of time kept ticking faster and faster. It took my parents... and then him. Now, here I am. Empty, waiting."

She sighed deeply.

"But I have you now. To talk to. To take care of me. To do everything for me. If not, maybe I'd have ended up in some old age home. Or worse, left in a temple courtyard."

She touched Radha's hand and smiled gently.

"That love... it's a blessing from a previous birth, I believe. Now, I only have one prayer — that I am never bedridden, waiting endlessly for death to come."

Radha didn't reply. Her throat was tight. She looked at Amma's eyes — still sharp despite the tears behind them — and wondered what her own fate would be.

She didn't know. Fate writes in silence, and they were all just readers waiting for the next line. And in that quiet night, two women sat — one at the dusk of life, the other watching the sun still high — holding space for each other between the pages of time.

5
Impulse

It was evening. The sun was sinking slowly behind the horizon, spreading a warm, golden hue over the restless waves. The beach was quiet except for the whisper of the wind and the rhythmic crash of the sea. A man sat alone on the sand, lost in thought.

Then, a scream tore through the calm.

He turned sharply. A woman — wild-haired, barefoot — was sprinting toward the ocean. Her movements were chaotic, as though she were trying to outrun the weight inside her. He ran after her, heart pounding, catching up just as she reached the edge of the surf.

He grabbed her arm. "Wait, What are you doing?"

She struggled to free herself. Her eyes were swollen with tears. "Let me go! I want to end it! I'm done!"

The waves crashed against them. Cold, violent. Real.

She collapsed to her knees in the wet sand, sobbing. Her pain was raw, like something she had held in too long. He knelt beside her, unsure of what to do, only knowing he couldn't walk away.

For a while, they said nothing. The sun dipped lower, casting long shadows and rays on her fair skin making it more beautiful. His heart wandered through her body wanting to own it for a moment. She was going to end her life, and it would mean that she has still space for one more emotion to surrender to. He took her in his arms and quenched his thirst for love.

The waves had calmed, leaving behind only scattered foam and the fading roar of the sea. He moved quietly along the shore, retrieving her clothes that the tide had carried off. With gentle hands, he offered them back to her.

She wrapped herself in silence first — not just the clothes, but a stillness that felt heavier than the night falling around them.

He knelt beside her. "Tell me now," he said softly, not demanding, not pressing. "Why did you take this decision?"

She looked at the horizon, the sun now swallowed by the sea, and whispered into his ears, "I've been diagnosed with Aids."

The words were fragile, barely audible above the hum of the breeze. But they struck like thunder. He sat back, breath held, heart tightening.

He was stunned. Not confused. Not angry. Just still.

Her words hung in the air like sea mist, and everything within him turned to ash. The desires that had once stirred so wildly inside him were gone now, vanished like smoke after a fire. What remained was emptiness, not peace, but something quieter. A void where impulse used to be. His heart felt like scorched wood, burned out, hollow, yet strangely aware for the first time.

In the distance, a dog howled. The sound floated across the shoreline, distant but piercing, and it echoed through him like a mirror, a voice carrying the shape of his own greed, and his shame.

And maybe that was the beginning of something. Not redemption. But truth.

6
Lords' Mercy!

It was late. Suma was cleaning the kitchen after dinner. It was raining, soft, steady, and unhurried. The drops pattered against the windows and roof, a gentle rhythm that filled the silence.

From the guest room, her aunt's snores rose and fell in uneven rhythms, like an old ceiling fan struggling against rusted hinges. She had come all the way from Palakkad, to see the lord and offer her prayers at the temple. Tired and worn from the travel, old age and stress, she had dozed off.

Her son's daughter—twenty-eight and still unmarried—was a constant worry.

Then there was her daughter's son, always wheezing. The medicines helped, but the fear never really left.

And if that wasn't enough, there was Ammini, the neighbour—loud, bitter, and quarrelsome.

She wanted to go with Suma to the temple and had made three offerings to God, wrapped in devotion and desperation. One for her granddaughter's marriage. One for her grandson's health. And one to take away the bitterness that clung to her life like a shadow, to dissolve the enmity that had settled in her heart and home.

Suma turned off the kitchen lights, tiptoed down the hallway, dusted her night gown, tied her hair into a top bun and got ready to lie down. The doorbell rang continuously and startled her.

Who could that be at this late hour? Had she forgotten to close the gates?

She slowly moved the curtains. In the dim light of the moon, she could see a man with a suitcase. A car just moved out of their gate.

Who was that?

Ohh it was Venuveten! Her husband, who had returned to Dubai just two months ago!

In the past, holidays were planned and everyone would know if someone was coming from the Gulf, but now it was a new trend, a naughty way of surprising family and friends.

Suma hastily opened the door and hugged him. It was indeed a surprise, and she was happy beyond words. She couldn't believe what she saw. Was it a dream or was it real!

But!

A sudden flash of darkness shook her. It was 10.45 pm, the time Dinesh used to call her.

Ohh God! What to do!

It was in the recent days that she had joined their school alumni group in WhatsApp, that got her re connected to Dinesh. She had always admired him in college. His smile and his winking eyes were her favourites about him. But she did not dare to talk to him about her love or admiration and had suffocated the desire deep down in her heart.

She only had one prayer now, that she wanted to be her Venuveten's forever.

Why did you come into my heaven again! Ohh God! What a stress!

"Venuveta, did you eat something" Suma asked coming out off the shock.

"Yes. I had two dosa from Kuttapetens shop on the way. Come lets sleep"

Venu drank some water and went to bed. Suma silenced her phone, neatly hid it under the cot and slid into the warmth and comfort of his arms. Don't know how long they slept, but she woke up hearing aunties call.

"What is she doing in the room, why did you lock the door? Wake up" Aunty did not know that Venu had come. It was a surprise for her as well.

"Venuveta, wake up. Ottapalam Aunty is here, she wants to go to the temple with us, get ready" Suma called out, and despite the body pain and tiredness, she had a shower. She wore a traditional Kerala saree and by the time she got ready Venu also woke up and was all set for the temple.

As planned, Ani came with his auto, and they started.

A cool breeze drifted through the early morning air, rustling the trees and sending a shiver through her that reminded her of his embrace the previous night, warm and quiet and unexpected.

The temple was busy as always. Bells rang in the distance, echoing off stone walls, and the scent of incense hung thick in the humid morning air. Devotees moved in slow lines, some with offerings of flowers and coconuts, others with only folded hands and whispered prayers.

As they entered through the security gate, a uniformed guard stepped forward and raised a hand. "Mobile phones not allowed inside," he said, pointing at the phone in Suma's hand.

Just then, another guard blocked Venu, who had been trailing behind, yawning.

"You cannot go inside with pants," the guard said firmly. "Go and wear a dhothi. Rules are rules." Venu blinked, caught off guard.

Immediately, Venu grabbed the phone from her hand.

"You both go inside and come," he said casually. "I can come even tomorrow. I'll just message everyone that I've arrived." He said waving Suma's phone.

Suma froze. Her breath caught in her throat. "Hmm," she managed, her voice barely audible.

Her mind screamed. *How could she have handed him the phone,* that held every insane, impulsive, desperate message exchanged with Dinesh. Late-night chats and words that didn't belong to a woman like her. She hadn't deleted them. Not even one

Her heart pounded like a drum trapped inside a box. Her skin turned cold. Everything seemed to blur...the people, the sounds, even the temple itself.

"Let's go! We have to offer prayers!" her aunt yelled, tugging her arm, already halfway through the temple gates.

Suma stumbled forward, her feet moving without consent. The stone beneath her soles felt hard and far away. *What prayers? What offerings?*

She didn't remember what she had come for. Her head throbbed; her chest tightened. Everything inside her felt broken, desecrated. Guilt and fear, layered like smoke, choking her from within. She was blank. She was lost.

And at any moment, she felt she might faint from the fear of what he might see. Of what he might know.

She remembered Valsala, the woman who was once known for her beauty, married to a businessman and settled in Dubai. From nothing to being a prominent face on stage and entertainments, that brought her high ego and attitude. Did some massive blunder on WhatsApp that was caught by her husband and deported back home after visa cancellation.

What a shame! Will she also suffer the same fate!

Can't even think. Ohh God! What a fate!

"Krishna, my lord, have mercy on me" That was the scream within her in the deep silence of the gushing blood within her.

"Dear, what's wrong with you?" her aunt asked, glancing back with concern. "I don't understand. Come now—we have to see the deity before we step outside the gates."

But Suma heard none of it. No rules. No beliefs. No thoughts. Her ears were ringing, her mouth dry. All she knew was one thing—*she had to get back to Venu. Now.*

Without answering, she turned and pushed through the crowd, her steps turning frantic. She brushed past the crowd; her breath came in bursts.

And then—there he was.

Venu, standing near the outer wall of the temple, laughing, completely at ease. He was talking to someone—Murali Krishnan, the son of their neighbour Kavallakkal Achu Nair. The two were smiling, mid-conversation, heads tilted in easy familiarity.

Suma stopped, her chest heaving, her whole-body trembling. The sight of her phone in Venu's hand felt like a burning coal. Her world narrowed down to that moment, that device, and the unspoken secrets it held inside.

"Ohh, Suma! You're back so fast?" Venu said with a chuckle, spotting her as she ran toward him. "I knew it. I was talking to him and forgot to send the messages."

He held up the phone casually, not even glancing at the screen.

Suma stopped short. She stared at him, trying to read his face.

Nothing. No change. No sharpness in his tone.

"Murali, how come you're here?" Suma asked, still catching her breath. "You were an atheist, weren't you?"

Murali smiled, a little sheepishly. "No, chechi"

Then his eyes softened, voice dropping just a bit.

"Whatever we believe, when real stress comes—when it presses down—we all end up calling him. Even if we don't say it aloud. Just having a glance at him... Krishna, who carries burdens, who heals all stress... it helps."

Okay, Suma, let's go," Venu said, slipping the phone back into her bag without a second thought. "We'll buy a few sarees for Aunty—after a tea, of course."

Aunty was a few steps away, busily examining a rack of brightly coloured toys for her grandchildren.

"See you, Murali," Venu called over his shoulder.

Murali raised a hand in farewell, his usual boyish smile lingering as he turned toward the temple.

As they walked away, Suma looked back once more. Her heart felt lighter, her breath steadier. *Was it you, my Krishna? Was it really you?* The panic still echoed faintly in her chest, but something greater had taken its place—relief, yes, but also awe.

Had the Lord Himself come down to protect her, to shield her shame?Murali, you are my God... my saviour, she thought silently, lips not moving, but heart crying out in gratitude.

She felt Venu's hand in hers—solid, warm, and steady. She clasped it gently, with new awareness. As they stepped into Hotel Ramakrishna, the aroma of filter coffee and the ghee roast welcoming them, she knew within his arms, within his trust, *lay her paradise.*

Krishna! Your mercy! Your magic!

7
Love, it seems!

"**I** am in love with you," he said, voice trembling—not from fear, but from the unbearable weight of truth.

"In deep love. You are haunting me day and night. I cannot eat. I cannot sleep. I have everything—yet I am empty. I have nothing, nothing but this love for you."

She stared at him. Silent. Stunned.

She was at the edge of old age—softly, gently passing into the twilight years. She had long stopped looking in mirrors. What was the use? The lipsticks were dry. The perfumes had gathered dust. The kajal had faded into memory. Now, there were only prayer beads and temple bells. Only silence, incense, and the slow, rhythmic chime of time passing. And now—this. A man, with fire in his eyes. Asking for love.

At first, she thought it was a cruel joke.

When she first started talking to him, it was just sympathy. A soft pull.

But soon, it became more. She found herself drawn to his wounds, to his loneliness, to the emptiness that wrapped around him. She put aside her hesitation, her fears, even her years.

She dusted the old mirror one morning. It had stood ignored for years in the corner of her bedroom. She looked at herself— truly looked—and for the first time in decades, she smiled.

"He wasn't lying," she whispered. "I am beautiful." She wanted to see him in flesh. And they finally met under a full moon sky. It was as if spring had come to a barren land. He kissed her, head to toe, warming every forgotten part of her.

They met again. And again. Under many more moonlit nights, woven in passion and rediscovery.

But seasons turn.

And with each meeting, she began to sense it. Something subtle, then obvious. The brightness in his eyes dimmed. The pauses grew longer. The laughter faded. The doors of

his excitement began to close—quietly, but surely. She watched them shut, one by one, with a heart that already knew.

And one night, the truth came: "You are not the one I imagined."

There it was. Cold, bare, and final. The intoxication of love had left him. She had feared this. Or maybe she had always known. That this love would not last. That it would stop mid-song. And now, it had.

Love, it seems. Love.

She looked at the mirror—and laughed.

A sharp, sudden laugh. Not bitter, not broken. Just... free.

She wiped the face he had once hungrily admired, smudging away the traces of his longing. Then, without hesitation, she closed her eyes tight. And in that moment, threw him carelessly, without ceremony or prejudice, out of her heart.

She crushed his memories like brittle ash between her fingers and let them float into the air—weightless, meaningless.

She swept her mind clean.

And deep within her, something began to burn—a fire like the smoldering of a corpse, final and irreversible.

The scent of incense filled the room, curling around her like smoke in a sanctum. She laid a white cloth over his memories, that were final. She buried them without tears, without a grave.

And then—She locked her heart.

Locked the love that had once danced wildly within it.

She found a lock that could never be opened again.

And flung the keys into the endless, indifferent sky.

8
Manju's Father

The unexpected off-season rain had silenced the usual AC whirrs in Sharjah. The city, wrapped in an unfamiliar chill, slept peacefully beneath a blanket of morning dew. The bone-piercing cold and the cozy warmth of my own blanket had lulled me into a deep, comforting sleep.

"Geetha,"A sudden voice pierced through my slumber. It was familiar—so achingly familiar—that it dragged me from the depths of my dreams.

Mohanettan was asleep beside me, breathing softly. I crawled out of bed without disturbing him, moved to the window, and slid the glass open.

Outside, the city was a blur of silver and stillness. The roundabout near the clock tower had a few cars circling quietly under orange streetlamps, and the moon was slowly settling in the sky with a quiet kind of beauty. Yet, something deeper stirred within me.

That voice. It called not just my name—it called my past.

And then it struck me. Like a forgotten photo falling out of a book.

It was Manju's father.

Some memories are like shadows behind curtains—hidden, but never gone. They wait quietly until a moment like this—a voice, a smell, a rain—to rush in like a reel of old film. Truth returns in celluloid: people, sounds, and expressions the heart stores even when the mind lets go.

And now, you'll have to come with me—to God's Own Country. To Kerala, where my memories live.

A land of innocence, overflowing like a nirapara on harvest day—brimming with truth, kindness, and the warmth of timeless love. A place wrapped in rivers, valleys, and temple bells; where every past moment holds a mirror to who I once was.

Let's begin with Manju.Like Mohanettan says—the girl with the big, lovely eyes. The girl who once knew me better than I knew myself.

She lives in Thrissur now, with her husband and two children. We don't talk much. Life has placed us in different corners of the world—but the bond remains, silent and strong.

Whenever I visit home, Manju comes to see me. And in every conversation, she used to mention her parents—especially her father. I had never met them, but through her stories, I knew everything. Her mother wasn't keeping well, she had said. So this time, during my trip to India, I decided I would go see them before Manju came to see me.

I took my neighbor, amma whom we call Ammachi, along and went to their home. They were staying with their son's family at the time.

Manju's mother opened the door. Ammachi introduced me: "This is Geetha, from Sharjah."

Manju's mother smiled. And then, from inside, I heard that voice again:

"Is that Geetha? Come inside!"

I quickly placed the fruits and snacks I had brought on the table and hurried toward the room. There he was—Manju's father—adjusting his mundu, struggling to get up from the bed in excitement. That sight has never left my mind.

"Turn on the lights," he told his wife. "The room is still dark. I can't see Geetha—let me see her once."

His wife gently whispered to me, "He cannot see. His high sugar took away his vision a few months ago." In his excitement to see me, he had forgotten he was blind.

He was the most gracious host I had ever seen. Despite his blindness, he commanded the room like the head of the family and offered hospitality with a kind of warmth I had never experienced.

"Check if that plantain is ripe," he told Manju's mother. "Give it to Geetha to take back with her."

He spoke to me as if we had known each other forever. "Geetha, did you go for the wedding at Vadakkanchery? The next one is on September 11th in Trivandrum, right?"

I was shocked. He listed every date—when I had arrived, where I'd been, what I was planning, even my return date. Every detail I had casually shared with Manju, he remembered—word for word, with exact dates.

It wasn't just memory—it was love. And what surprised me was the kind of love a father shares with his daughter. And in that moment, I saw how deeply Manju and her father were connected—friends who shared everything.

I left that day feeling honoured and embraced in a way I hadn't expected. I promised to return soon.

That evening, when Mohanettan called, I shared everything with him. He was just as moved, and said he would love to meet them during our next visit to Kerala.

Days passed. After all my holiday plans, I returned to Sharjah. And soon enough, three months later, another trip to Kochi came up—this time, with Mohanettan.

As we passed through Kunumburam on the way home from the airport, I suddenly remembered Manju's father. I told Mohanettan we should visit them in a day or two.

The next morning, our neighbour Ammachi came to see me. She looked tired and weak. When I asked, she sighed, "I've been traveling... mentally worn out."

In the middle of her usual gossip, she dropped the news: "Manju's father passed away."

I froze.

"He asked about you when I visited him—just days before he died," she said gently.

I couldn't believe it. The man I had promised to see again... was gone "It's been one and a half months," she added. "You hadn't called for a while, so I couldn't tell you."

My heart ached. A deep, quiet grief settled in.

Some relationships aren't built by blood—they're built by heart. They cling like cold flesh, silent and firm.

A few days later, I met Manju. I told her everything—how much her father had respected me, how he had remembered every little thing I shared.

In a world where old age homes are marketed like resorts, people like Manju are rare gems. I told her, "Had I known he cared so much, I would have come earlier, Manju."

She nodded, eyes brimming "I used to share everything with him. I still talk to him. I sit by his empty chair and tell him everything. I know he listens. I just can't accept he's gone."

Her eyes shed tears, and I could feel it. Her grief matched mine.

The cold breeze hit my face, and the dew of memory stirred something deep in me. I closed the window.

I turned to find Mohanettan awake, the bedside light glowing.

He looked at me, concerned. "What's troubling you?"

"Manju's father," I whispered.

He understood without needing further explanation. He always does.

"Come, let's sleep. It's almost dawn," he said, gently patting my shoulder.

I couldn't sleep right away. Memories haunted me. But his comforting touch slowly invited sleep back to my eyelids like an old friend.

The next morning, I woke late.

Mohanettan had a meeting, so he had quietly slipped out to the office early that morning. I sat up in bed, tired and drowsy. His diary was on the table beside me, and a note on top of it caught my attention:

"I've kept a scale inside the diary as a bookmark. Read it."

Curious, I removed the scale and opened the page.

"I started walking through the roads described by Geetha. A path marked by the footsteps of a father. A path familiar to me only through her words.

I walked through that unfamiliar way without fear, without hesitation. I had to ask for directions, but when I arrived— it was as if I had stepped into a memory more vivid than Geetha's description.

The creepers, the trees, the birds... everything looked like it had been waiting for me. Through the greenery, I saw the house crowned with roofing tiles, just as she had described. I stepped inside slowly, wondering what relationship I truly had with these people.

Sunlight scattered like golden confetti across the path—a warm welcome only nature can give. I carried something within me, an emotion I couldn't name. A tightness in my chest, a gentle suffocation.

Then, like a blessing, a ripe mango fell at my feet, carried by the breeze. I smiled—Geetha had once mentioned making mango curry on our next visit.

She was there—Manju's mother—frail, tired, but somehow glowing. As soon as she heard Geetha's name, her face lit up like a child's. In an instant, she transformed into a woman of stories, laughter, and kindness.

She held my hand, called me 'son', and her eyes swelled with tears. She didn't ask the question I could feel hanging between us—why didn't I bring Geetha?—but she spoke instead of how much her husband had longed to see her once more. I could see her heart melt in sorrow with every word.

Geetha was right—people here know only how to love.

I sat with her for a while, then stood to leave. She walked with me to the doorstep, and stood there, unmoving, until I vanished from her view.

I had gone there without a reason, but when I returned, I carried a truth within me: there was another family—one that had been waiting for me all along. A family that knew me before I ever knew them. A family that expected me, welcomed me, and gave me love I never asked for but deeply needed."

It took me a while to come back to myself. I wasn't sure if what I had just read was real, or a beautiful figment of Mohanettan's imagination. But one thing was certain—he had loved that family, deeply. As if from another life.

And because I experienced it with my own heart, I have come a long way, still writing about it.

9
Poison Pen Letter

"Did you know why Surendran's youngest daughter, Rukhu, was running around like that, shaking her body, Meenakshi?"

"Oh, I saw her," said Meenakshi, eyes lighting up. "The moment I saw her skipping down the lane, full of sparkle, I knew something was up. I didn't waste time. My phone was on zero balance, but I recharged it immediately. I *had* to call Sharadha"

"My heart was wobbling without knowing why," she added. "I felt like I would burst. And you know my sister-in-law — the one my brother ran away with, as if there were no other women in this village? She wouldn't let me sleep until we found out the truth. But would Sharadha call back? Never. So I called again."

"Don't change the topic," I said, leaning closer. "Tell me what you heard."

"The girl has a proposal," Meenakshi whispered. "From a boy down South. A *Gulf boy*! They say he earns almost four lakh rupees a month!"

I gasped. "Four lakh? Per month?"

"Per month," Meenakshi confirmed, nodding. "They met through some Instagram or something. The girl, Rukhu, she knew how to work boys, it seems. He fell for her just like that. And guess what? The marriage was fixed within two days. Two days!"

"She must've danced with joy," I muttered.

"She did! And that boy, he sent her gifts even before marriage.
Chocolates, imported perfume and even fairness cream for
her mother!"

"For her *mother*?" I almost choked.

"Yes! Maybe he thought, brighten the family, brighten the
future!"

We laughed, shaking our heads. But only a few days later, I found Meenakshi again, and her face wasn't smiling.

"Where were you all these days, Meenakshi?" I asked.

"I lost the paper where I had written your number," I said. "Must have gone into the fire. But I've been dying to talk to you. Something's wrong with Rukhu. She's lost so much weight, her face has lost all light. She doesn't even smile anymore."

"What happened?" I asked, heart sinking.

Meenakshi looked around, then leaned in.

"I haven't slept, I swear," she said. "I keep tossing and turning. My husband Raghavetten asked me yesterday if I've gone mad. *'I work all day. I can only satisfy you so much. What is it you keep muttering about at night?'* he said."

"What could I tell him?" Meenakshi sighed. "That my head is breaking without these stories? That without gossip, I don't know how to rest?"

"Tell me what happened."

Meenakshi paused, eyes wide.

"Ohh, you don't know?" she said. "The wedding... has been called off."

"What? Why?"

"Someone wrote a poison letter to the boy's parents," she whispered. "Said Rukhu had *bad character*. That she was seen many times with her friend's husband. No name on the letter. No address. Just filth on a folded piece of paper."

"What a world," I said, feeling cold inside.

"Yes. And the worst part? They *believed* it. Just like that. No questions. No proof. Only the weight of gossip and suspicion."

We sat in silence, the story settling in the air like dust. The laughter from before had disappeared. The excitement, the four lakh rupees, the perfume, the fairness cream — it all felt like someone else's dream.

People still believe letters written by cowards — people who don't even sign their names. One anonymous sentence, and a girl's entire future is blown to ashes.

10
Puberty

Every year, the youth festival is my favourite part of school. I live for it. The music, the lights, the buzz in the corridors. Usually, I'm sprinting from one stage to another, trying to catch every performance. I want the front row, always. I cheer like it's my job, soak in every beat, every move, like it's all meant for me.

But today... I don't know what happened.

I saw him.

I see him every day. Nothing special. Until now.

But today, I couldn't look away.

I should've been watching the dancers. They were magic on stage—spinning, glowing, the crowd clapping—but I wasn't even there. Not really. I was stuck on him. His uneven teeth, the way his eyes look a little tired, like they carry stories. His laugh that I somehow never really noticed until now. He's not even doing anything—just sitting, talking, being normal. But everything in me feels different.

Why now?

Why, of all days, when everything I love is happening around me, and I am lost in thoughts of him? I don't get it.

I want to enjoy the festival. I want to feel like myself again—loud, excited, all over the place. But I feel like I'm floating outside of the crowd, watching him and wondering what the hell happened to me.

There was a little catch in my stomach, a cramp that came out of nowhere. I shifted in my seat, trying to ignore it, still watching him.

And then I felt it. A little wetness. A strange awareness low in my body. A breeze passed through the open hall. It touched my skin and carried with it the faint, metallic scent of blood.

I didn't move. I didn't even fully understand.

She did not know that her body was growing, it was shifting somewhere between girlhood and something else entirely.

Years rolled by like film reels speeding through a projector—too fast to grasp. School ended, and so did that whirlwind of festivals, crushes, secrets whispered behind textbooks. One by one, we all walked away from that old building, stepping into our own stories. Careers, marriages, heartbreaks, children... even grandchildren. Life unfolded with all its strangeness.

Then one day, we came back.

A reunion. The same school, same corridors, now faded and quiet. We were older, with lines on our faces and laughter that came more softly. We gathered in the hall. And there he was—him. The same uneven teeth, the same soggy eyes that once made my heart race.

He came and sat beside me, just like that. And I... felt nothing.

Not disappointment, not regret, not even nostalgia. Just quiet.

What had happened to me? Where was that fire, that ache?

Was this another stage of life, like puberty? Was this what it was meant to grow older as a woman?

Not sadness. Not emptiness. Just a feeling of maturity.

Had I outgrown womanhood the same way I outgrew adolescence? Was this yet another turning, like the first drop of blood on a school day that told me I was becoming something new?

But this time, there was nothing but just a faint memory of that smell—metallic, warm, alive.

Maybe it's just another phase, where desire is replaced by memory, and emotion by understanding. Where we no longer chase meaning in every glance or heartbeat. Maybe it's not the end, but a turning toward something else.

Was this the sunset of the womanhood in me?

11
She was always like that!

Yes, she had always been this way, ever since I first knew her.

So why, Pankajachechi, are you talking about her like that now?

You say she's changed. But I knew her—really knew her—far better than you ever did.

Back then, she had nothing. She wore old sarees, their faded dots and frayed patterns barely clinging to fabric donated by others. Her blouses were always too loose, handed down without care for fit or comfort. Her body was all bone—thin, starved. Her underskirt never stayed on her hips, so she'd wrap her saree in two tight folds just to keep it in place. The torn frills of her petticoat would flutter ahead of her as she walked.

And yet—what grace she carried. That slender frame held a quiet beauty, her bosom and hipline carved like sculpture, delicate but strong. She was radiant in a way only hardship can shape.

She was so kind. So gentle.

The marks her husband left on her face—his gifts of anger—were always visible. Like blueprints. But she smiled through them, meeting everyone she passed with warmth in her eyes and grace in her steps.

She never complained. Never told her sorrow to anyone. She simply smiled.

And when we joked and laughed, she would cover her mouth with all her fingers and smile shyly—so soft, so full of life. No bangles on her wrists, no rings on her fingers, but her hands had their own language. Her eyes spoke the rest.

And now, you say she's changed.

You say her son got a job—high up in the Navy—and that's why she's different. You say she went to Delhi with him and came back full of pride. You say she laughs behind her jewelled hands now—just to show off.

But why, Pankajachechi? Why talk about her like this?

If you had looked at her closely back then, truly seen her, you would've noticed her sunken belly, her cracked lips, the hunger wrapped in silence. You would've seen the dignity she wore when life gave her none.

And maybe then, today, you wouldn't speak of her with such judgment.

She was always like that. Even back then, when she had nothing.

12
It was him!

He was in my usual way—or maybe, because he was there, it became my way.

I used to notice him, search for him in every crowd. If I didn't see his face, I felt incomplete, like I'd drifted off track. I never needed to speak to him. Just the sight of his face gave me joy. I didn't need conversation. I didn't need him to smile. Just seeing him filled some quiet, aching part of me I didn't even know existed until he was there.

But he never noticed me. He seemed untouched by my presence, unaware I even existed. He never looked back. His eyes passed over me like I was   part of the background—nothing more than a shadow, maybe a passerby. But for me, seeing him was enough.

That day, I couldn't go. I didn't feel like it. I felt weak. I couldn't get out of bed. I felt drained, like my limbs were too heavy and my chest too full of something I couldn't name.

What was wrong with me?
It didn't take long to realize—he was the reason.

It was as if all the colour had drained from the world. The thought of walking that path, of possibly not seeing him—or worse, seeing him and him not seeing me—felt unbearable.

Love, or whatever I felt, shouldn't be like this. It shouldn't make me feel this hollow, this small. It should come freely—not as a constant ache, not something I had to *beg the universe* for. I pulled my blanket over my face, trying to push away the weight pressing down on me.

I had never failed anywhere in life. But now, in front of the love I carried for him, I felt like a cheap failure. My mind spun, my body restless.

I had never failed like this in front of anyone. But somehow, in front of *him*, I had collapsed. Not because he rejected me. He hadn't even noticed me enough to reject.

I felt like a ghost, haunting my own story.

I grabbed my phone, looking for distraction, scrolling through old, unseen messages.And then one message stopped me in my tracks.

From an unknown number.
Nameless.
"Where are you? I was waiting for you for a long time."

I blinked. Rubbed my eyes. Read it again. Again. Was it real?

My heart pounded, joy crashing over me like a wave.

My body, moments ago limp and lifeless, surged with energy. I sat up in bed, alive with a joy so sharp it almost hurt. Everything felt new—reborn. And In I felt like dancing to the rhythm of love that was in front of me.

Yes, it was from him.
It was *him*.

13
The Bird Cage

I wanted to meet you. If I couldn't meet you, I would have traced you down somehow. I had your name, your silence, your shadow burned into my thoughts. I would've found the corners of the earth you hid in. But you slipped away faster than I could run.

I wanted to look at you straight into your eyes and tell you everything. But I was late. Too late.

I knew him—long before you knew him, long before the blunder that pulled you into his darkness.

But I couldn't tell you. How could I? I couldn't even meet you, let alone call. I held onto words like smuggled secrets in my chest, choking on them every time I almost reached out.

Then you went away doing the biggest stupidity anyone can do!

You went away in the most final way a person can go. You left without a message, without noise—just silence and the cold weight of your decision echoing in our lives.

I was there among the school kids who got permission to see you for the last time as you lay wrapped in a coarse mat, lifeless and still, in front of the Mortuary of the Government hospital.

What was I supposed to say to that?

What do you say to a piece of lifeless flesh that used to laugh, cry, dream, ache?

What do you say when the only words you ever had for someone never left your mouth?

I stood there, staring.

But what you wanted came true.

Your mother is suffering, insane with grief at your loss. Her world has collapsed.

You were her only child. Her only reason. You were the dream she carried through every struggle, every long night, every sacrifice. And then you were gone.

The grief has locked her in, and the world has learned not to push too hard. She isn't angry. She isn't violent. She's just... gone into trauma

She had a good job, a respectable position, but all gone with you. Time can't touch her. She is not living in it anymore.

And you hung yourself on her khadi saree? Horrible!

And all because she locked you at home, to stop you from running away with him, that good for nothing man?

What a revenge!

I met him a week before I travelled here, at the airport.

He looked cool. Confident. That new-gen style—an ear stud, styled hair, a casual sharpness in his walk. Like life had been good to him lately.

By his side was a beautiful woman, his wife. And there were two little girls too. Tiny, bright-eyed, his children.

He told me, it was a love marriage. All happened in a year, after you left.

What love was that?

What kind of love ends so quietly, so quickly, so cleanly?

And what were you to him then? Just a season? A phase?

I always remembered you.

Not just your voice or your laugh, but the tiny things. Your birdcage earrings, the ones you wore with everything. Your favourite.

And that tooth. That one slightly unaligned little tooth that made your smile imperfect, and somehow even more beautiful because of it. I used to watch it when you laughed, how your whole face lit up, how the earrings would dance with you, catching the light like they were laughing too.

Do you remember that day, during the drill session?

You turned to me so casually, as if it was nothing, and said,"How beautiful is that eyeliner on your eyes."

No one had ever said that to me before. Not like that. Not with that much truth.

And strangely, no one ever has since.

Maybe that's why I remember you so much. Not just for the big things, but for that single sentence, it settled into me like an admiration.

And now, every time I look in the mirror, every time I trace that same line across my eyelids, I hear your voice again.

I see those birdcage earrings swinging with your laugh, that colored bindi resting like a thought between your brows, that smile, that calmness.

Everything about you still clings to me. just to remind me you were real.

Now like you, I am also here, not by stupidity, but fate.

I wanted to live, I had dreams, I never wanted to come here so soon. And it happened within a flash of a moment.

It burns me inside when I see you sitting like a culprit with your heads shook in shame. I cannot bear this.

I don't know, if there is a rebirth. I am not sure, but if it happens, let this be a lesson to you...

And now, every time I look in the mirror, every time I trace that same line across my eyelids, I hear your voice again.

14
The Devoted Love

The morning sunlight filtered in through the thin curtains, drawing long streaks across the floor. I sat on the edge of the bed, motionless, staring at nothing.

Why did you love me so much?

Why did you hurt me so deeply?

Even today, the pain goes down to my bones — sucking out the juices of life and leaving me dry. No matter how much I try, I can never forget you. Your thoughts cling to my heart like spider webs.

"Wha are you thinking, my dear?" came the soft voice of Devakiyamma.

Her voice startled me. I hadn't noticed her come in, hands full of freshly washed laundry.

Her presence broke through the silence. I turned.

"Ohh, my Devakiyamma... you washed that too?" I asked, my voice catching slightly in my throat.

There, in the folds of white sheets, was a faint, persistent stain — red, blurred at the edges. It had never quite washed out.

From the day we met, he had only ever praised my hands... my fingers, my painted nails. That was the one thing he admired until the very end.

He used to say I had the most graceful fingers. He loved the red polish. Said it made me look powerful, radiant. Even when we fought. Even when the words between us turned cold. He would still glance at my hands, the polish shining like rubies, and soften.

And when he bid farewell, he looked into my eyes without blinking — even then, he held my hands close to his heart

It had been a small moment — the kind you think you'll forget. But it clung to me.

I have not forgotten.

That night, the phone rang like a scream in the silence. The voice on the other end stumbled, fractured. I heard the words but not their meaning.

I fainted and when I opened my eyes, the world was altered. I remember the prayer that came from the pit of my soul, wordless and raw. Let it not be true. Let it be a mistake. A cruel joke. Please, God, please...

But it was true. He was gone. Like a flame snuffed out by wind. And I was left in the dark, grasping at smoke.

"Why did you do this to me, God?" I cried into the emptiness. "What sin have I committed? I haven't even harmed an ant in my life..."

Why did that vehicle come roaring?

Why did you look away for just one second?

Or was that too because of me?

I had filled his dreams with my love. Painted them in red. And now that red would always remind me of him — not as joy, but as ache.

Devakiyamma moved quietly around the room, placing folded clothes in neat piles. She said nothing.

Devakiyamma, you don't know my agony. Neither you, nor anyone else, can understand this pain.

Even time cannot erase his face from my heart.

His face is etched into my memory, carved deep like stone weathered by centuries of longing.

And it will stay — a beautiful, bleeding memory — until my final breath.

15
The Dog and Richie

She had no wealth. She was not rich. Yet, people called her *Richie*. That was her nickname—not for the coins in her pocket, but for the treasure in her heart.

The name wasn't given because of wealth—it was because of who she was. Richie had something rarer than gold: a heart that beat for others.

From a young age, she had an unusual instinct to help. Even with nothing in her hands, she would still try to ease someone's burden. If a friend was in need, she would offer the little money she had saved for herself.If a stranger was hungry, she would give away her meal.

Her helping nature grew with her age. As time passed, Richie gave away more than just small saving. She began selling the things she owned. Clothes, furniture, anything that could bring relief to someone else's pain. She believed that the tears of joy she saw in others were the greatest blessing she could receive.

But years rolled on, and eventually, the savings ran out. Her body began to grow weak, her health deteriorated. Still, she gave what she could, her time, her presence, her strength. Until, one day, even that was no longer possible.

When her persistent cough grew worse, she visited a doctor. The diagnosis came heavy: Tuberculosis!

And with that, the final curtain seemed to fall.

The same people who once embraced her generosity now avoided her. They turned their faces, crossed the street, closed their doors. Those who had once clung to her kindness now cast her aside like a forgotten page.

Alone and shunned, Richie withdrew into her home, a small space that echoed with silence. She longed to talk. To laugh. To simply be *seen*. But no one came.

Days blurred into nights. The air grew heavier. Until one day, a faint, scratching sound came from the door.

She had a visitor.

There, barely able to stand, was a stray dog.Mud caked his fur. His ribs pushed against his skin. But his eyes looked at her with recognition.

She remembered him. He was the same dog she had fed from time to time, offering biscuits when she had nothing else.She had never expected anything in return. But here he was.

He had come back.

With slow steps, shaking the mud off his body, the dog entered the house and lay beside her. He wagged his tail softly as she spoke. He listened as she whispered her thoughts, her memories, her loneliness.

And in the final days of her life, Richie was not alone.

No one else came. No neighbours, no friends. But that dog. the one soul who remembered her kindness, stayed.

His loyalty became her comfort. His presence, her peace.

He stayed by her side until her last breath, his eyes never leaving hers, his tail still wagging, as if to tell her that she mattered to him.

16
The Ecstacy

On her way to college, the beggar's image became an almost permanent fixture in her daily routine. Each morning, as she walked the familiar path, her eyes would inevitably drift toward him—an insane man, sitting on the benches of the tea stall, a silent observer of the world passing by. His long hair tangled like a wild forest, his beard scraggly and unkempt, his clothes ragged and worn by both time and weather. The cold of January would find him shivering, huddled close to himself, while the summer sun would scorch his skin, his frail frame casting no shade from the unforgiving heat. He just existed, in the space between the bustling world of commuters and the chaos of

city life, a ghost who seemed to fade into the surroundings as soon as he was seen. Yet, for her, he was never invisible.

There was something about his stillness that unsettled her. Every time her eyes met his, they would lock for a fleeting second, but his eyes would immediately shift away, retreating into the chaos of his mind. Top of FormBottom of Form

That day also like always she eagerly peeped at the tea stall but couldn't believe her eyes. She blinked again and again, to see if she could believe what she saw.

Her mind raced. How could this be? Just yesterday, he had been that wild, unkempt beggar, eyes filled with madness, shivering in the cold and burning in the sun. Now, here he was, among a group of laughing, carefree people, looking so different—clean-shaven, well-groomed, as if he belonged to another world altogether

How did that happen? She wondered.

May be the youngsters of the nearby club helped him, said her friend Divya, whose brother was one among them.

But she couldn't shake the feeling that something more was happening here. It was more than just a makeover. There was something in his eyes, something that had always been there, but now it seemed more intense, more real.

Their eyes again met. He looked straight into her eyes, without withdrawing. There was

something special in his looks and the way he looked at her. It sent a wave of kick inside her. There was a hunger to love and be loved in his mad eyes. After all love is a madness right! So, there is nothing madder than falling in love with a mad man and she welcomed him into her insane heart.

That night was theirs. The lunatic undressed himself and her, and as the night unfolded, their love blossomed in the quiet spaces between words. In the gentle touches and shared glances, they made love without limits, becoming one, caressing and smothering each other. It was a night of discovery, of vulnerability, of two souls intertwining in a way that felt both new and timeless.

They turned more sleepless nights into blissful moments of ecstasy. She welcomed his manliness, that flowed into her seeding a new life within, and it bloomed into a sweet little cry of a bundle of joy that was only theirs.

Life and love lingering together!

Sudden knocks and shouts on the door, awakened her. what was happening?

"The sun has come down and entered the room and still you are sleeping? Get up" the yelling noise. That should me mom!

She jerked and looked around; the naked beggar was not there. She also had her clothes on. She sat on her bed clinging on to the sweet dream that lazily caressed her.

The dream brought a smile on her lips. A kind of insane laughter swept her. Even though she was awake, his eyes had sunk into her chest so deep.

"Yes, I trust your eyes, it's my paradise, a; paradise that drives me crazy"

Her mother was screaming again, calling out for her, angrily.

With each breath, she embraced the mad man, the love, the nights and the dream, savouring the sweetness and the thrill it brought. Before her mother could break the pleasure of all that she was clinging onto, she walked out of her bed and opened the door.

And carrying the burden of the beautiful ecstasy and insane dreams in her eyes, she stepped out into a new dawn that welcomed her.

17
The Look

"What happened to you, Karthi? You've changed so much. There's a life in your eyes, in your look—something we've never seen before."

"What happened to me?" she smiled. "It seems I've gained more energy. That Ammalu asked me, Kunjirama." She chuckled.

"So, is it because of that? Even I noticed it. After that day, you've been different. Have you started using more eyeliner? Or maybe eating more betel leaves to add color to your lips?" he asked, half in jest, half in disbelief.

"I don't know, my Kunjirama," she said softly. "I've changed completely. Just last month, I was praying to die. But now... now I want to live."

He was quiet for a moment. Then he sighed.

"Hmm. "I loved you, you know," Kunjirama said suddenly. "I really did. For so long. But now it's too late. You have children. Grandchildren. And the hair on my chest—where I dreamed of holding you—has turned grey."

She looked at him, eyes shining.

He paused, his voice tinged with something between sorrow and affection.

"My Karthi, you've changed so much. But still, I carry your old image in my heart. You were the woman who seeded the emotion of love in me. Do you remember, when I came for your grandchild's annaprashan, and you served me food? Like a wife would serve her husband? Do you know how that felt to me? That day, I looked at you in awe. Do you know how much I had longed for that? That was why I gave you that look."

He poured his heart out.

Karthi looked away, her voice lower now.

There was a silence between them—gentle but heavy.

"That's all I ever wanted, my Kunjirama. That look... once in a while. Like the oil that keeps a lamp burning."

And for a brief moment, their age, their past, the world around them—none of it mattered. There was only the warmth between two hearts, long denied, finally speaking.

18
The Sacred Headgear

This is about the god himself.

Theyyam.

Theyyam, is a Hindu ritual art form performed in the Northern parts of South India. It culminates with the placement of the sacred headgear on the performers head, signifying the entrance of power within.

The performer, now transformed into a deity, moves among the gathered devotees, offering them blessings and purifying the space with sacred energy.

The performers of Theyyam undergo ardent fasting before the ceremony, embracing discipline forgetting hunger and thirst. After all, when immersed in deep divinity, hunger and thirst vanish into thin air. This act of fasting is not just a physical preparation but a spiritual purification, allowing the performer to connect deeply with the divine.

The burning emotions of the people gathered are understood and mirrored by Theyyam, who becomes a vessel to channel their collective hopes, fears, and desires.

Through this profound ritual, the deity brings comfort and solace, acknowledging the fervent prayers of the devotees.

Theyyam himself would keep its hands on each devotees head and shower blessings saying,

"I am there, I will take care of you, let you be blessed with all the goodness of the universe, you will know no difficulty"

The ones who received the blessings wiped their tears and moved aside.

At the end, until the last blessing was given to the last devotee, and with the help of four men when the hefty forty-two couplet sized crown, the "thirumudi" on the headgear was removed from the deity's head, the Theyyam did not realise its burden on him.

Because he was God himself!

And when the twenty-one layered headgear itself, embedded with twenty-one metallic stones was neatly removed and the divine makeup of the face was cleanly washed off, the Theyyam transformed back to its original human form, a common man.

Breaking his fast and the hunger that squeezed his stomach into himself, with just a tender coconut water, he walked with a humble smile, amongst the devotees taking leave for the day and the occasion.

As he bid farewell to the dispersing crowd and walked through them, paving way decently, even for the big vehicles to move smoothly, they did not even realise that he was the God to whom they sought blessings from, a few hours ago. He was now just an artist who was enacting what life was asking him to do for his daily bread.

He started walking home with nothing but a heart that was heavy with the burden that was awaiting him at home.

The groom's family would come home today to see his daughter.

Can he reach home on time?

What should he give them?

What did he have?

Nothing!

All that he had was a home that would be mortgaged by the bank any moment. A home that stood on rusted frames, broken walls and shattered dreams.

Without any decorations and polishes of life and with just a soul full of debts and fears of every tomorrow that lay ahead, he entered his home.

19
The Gold Coins

"The four gold coins I gave you to keep safe—please give them to me, Laksmikutty. I need them," Dakshayaniyamma said, her voice hoarse with urgency.

Could she really have ever had the means to entrust four gold coins to someone for safekeeping? Even the black thread around her neck was fraying, close to snapping. Still, she stood there and insisted, "What are you thinking? Go and get them."

From inside the house, in a soft, slow whisper, Sumathiyamma replied, "Don't give it to her, you fool. Those coins belong to Kunjiparvathy. She gave them to me years ago to keep safe, afraid her drunkard husband might sell them off. You know how many people come to us, asking to keep their belongings safe."

She paused, then added, "Just yesterday evening, I forgot everything for a moment and sat on the verandah wondering whose they were. I must have spoken it out loud. That liar Dakshayani must have heard me. I saw someone like her walking past my window. Ever since she was a child, she's had this filthy habit—sneaking around and listening to others' conversations."

Furious now, Sumathiyamma stormed out, her face ablaze with anger. She fixed Dakshayani with a fierce glare.

"Don't ever dare to come and stand in front of me like this again!" she snapped, before turning her back and slamming the door behind her.

Dakshayani stood there, head bowed in shame. Maybe it was poverty. Maybe it was the hard life, the humiliations stacked over the years like dry firewood, that had pushed her to this—towards dishonesty, towards despair.

20
Thiruvathira Fasting

"This time, I want to take the Thiruvathira fast," Dhanya declared with quiet determination.

Thiruvathira, an auspicious day in late December or early January, marks both the birthday of Lord Shiva and his divine union with Goddess Parvati. On this day, many women fast, offering prayers for the long life and health of their husbands. It is believed that sincere devotion on this day never goes unanswered.

Dhanya and her husband had recently moved into their new home, a little away from her ancestral place. Coincidentally—or perhaps by divine arrangement—there was a Shiva temple right next to their new house. She couldn't shake off the fear that ignoring the fast, especially with the temple so close by, might bring misfortune to her or her husband.

To do it right, she sought guidance from her neighbor, Thankam, about the rituals and customs.

On Thiruvathira day, she woke up early, lit the lamp with deep reverence, and prepared a simple porridge made from tender coconut water and arrowroot powder—traditionally taken on an empty stomach to begin the fast. After getting dressed in a new set of *mundu*, Kerala's traditional attire, she headed to the temple.

There, she made her offerings, praying earnestly on her husband's *nakshatra*—his birth star. Each ritual was carried out with care, her mind full of silent pleas and hope.

After completing the poojas, she went to collect the *prasadam*—the sacred offering of food. But to her surprise, the queue was unusually long. She stood at the very end, scanning the crowd to see if she could find a familiar face, someone to chat with and distract herself from the gnawing hunger. The porridge she had in the morning was hardly enough for her sturdy frame.

Leaning forward to catch sight of someone, she finally spotted Radhamani at the front—her neighbour, clutching the food slip. Radhamani looked like a monk—her forehead thick with ash and red *kumkum*, her face radiating fierce devotion.

A sharp pang of jealousy jabbed Dhanya. Her hunger couldn't accept the fact that Radhamani was so ahead in the line and that she would get her share of food before her.

But the feeling didn't last long.

Moments later, Radhamani stormed out of the line, her face flushed with rage and the receipt still clutched in her hand.

"It's not wheat, it's rice!" she shouted, livid. "All these years I've taken this fast and not once have I eaten anything made of rice on this day. What's the point if I eat it now? Then all of this—everything I'm doing for my husband—it'll all be for nothing!"

Dhanya was startled but quickly approached her.

"Ohh Radhamani, don't do this. It's already so late. Do you have the time to go home and cook something with wheat? And think—wouldn't refusing the *prasadam* be an insult to the temple? To Lord Shiva himself? He's the Lord of Destruction, remember. You don't want to make him angry."

Radhamani stared back for a moment—her fury softened into guilt. Like a scolded schoolgirl, she rejoined the queue.

The sun now stood high and harsh. The ash and *kumkum* on Radhamani's face had begun to melt, trickling down like war paint in surrender. My heart sank watching her—this woman who bore the heat, hunger, and hardship, all in silent sacrifice for her husband.

Little did Peethambaran know the lengths his wife went to, year after year,for his well-being.

And Dhanya knew something Radhamani didn't. Peethambaran, her husband—the very man for whom she was melting in the sun—was not the saint she thought he was.

Even last week, he had the audacity to flirt with me, his neighbour, whispering sweet words coated with sugar.

Only I knew it. *At least now, stop it, Peethambaran*, Dhanya thought bitterly.

21
Two Ladies

It was a Sunday morning, a day I always reserve for sleeping in. Wrapped snug in my blanket, I tried to squeeze in a few more minutes of sleep. But there was a lot to do that day, so after a bit of tossing and turning, I finally got up.

A quick shower and breakfast later, I was in the mood for some shopping. With a wedding coming up, my friend's daughter's, I thought it would be a good time to buy a nice silk saree for myself and one to gift the bride. I wanted something fresh in design, something unique.

One of the perks of living in town is the ease of access. no need to waste time hunting for an auto or planning ahead. By the time I had made up my mind, I was already at the nearest mall. Being a regular customer, I was familiar with the place and the people there.

I made my way straight to the second floor, to the saree section. After browsing for a while, I picked two lovely sarees from the new arrivals. As I was heading to the counter to pay, I heard a voice from behind.

"Madam," someone called.

I turned to see a strikingly beautiful woman, she was a promoter for a well-known cosmetics brand.

"Please try something, madam," she said sweetly.

I smiled and politely declined. "I don't need anything right now."

But she insisted again, "Please..."

There was something gentle about her—her smile, her request—it made me pause. I stayed for a moment to listen to her explain the products, even though I had no interest in them. I finally said, "I don't want any of these. I'm actually looking for a lipstick. Do you have one?"

Unfortunately, she didn't have the shade I wanted. "It's out of stock, madam. But I'll order it right away. It will be here in three days. Please share your number—I'll call you when it arrives."

I gave her my number and was about to leave when she followed me with another lipstick.

"This colour will suit you better, madam. There's no harm in trying something different. Just try this once—I'll put it on for you."

Though I wasn't convinced, I agreed hesitantly and let her apply it. As she did, she complimented me—"You have such beautiful lips, madam."

But when I looked in the mirror, I didn't quite like the shade.

"Just call me when you get the one I asked for," I said with a smile.

I paid for the sarees and left for home.

That night, just as I was winding down for bed, a message blinked onto my screen.

"Hi."

It was from the same promoter I'd met at the mall— the woman who had insisted I try on a lipstick and had complimented my lips with such quiet admiration.

I responded with a polite "Hello," not thinking much of it.

But from then on, it became a routine. Every day, she would send a message. Sometimes just a friendly greeting, sometimes a compliment. I replied when I could—never immediately, and never in depth. But without fail, at least once each day, her message would mention my lips. She seemed fascinated by them.

I brushed it off at first. Perhaps she was just being friendly, or perhaps that was her way of maintaining a connection for business. Either way, I didn't think too much of it.

Then another Sunday arrived, and with it came my usual indulgence—a lazy morning, meant for sleeping in. But that morning, the continuous *ping* of WhatsApp notifications broke the peace. Message after message kept lighting up my phone, one after the other. Irritated, I finally picked it up.

All were from her.

Her words, this time, felt... different. Longer, more personal. She wasn't talking about makeup anymore. She was describing me—my features, my expressions, my body. Always returning to my lips. There was a tone in her messages—something intense, something that made me pause.

I felt a tight discomfort in my chest. The kind that doesn't come from fear exactly, but from uncertainty. I didn't know how to respond. Part of me didn't even want to.

When I finally asked her why she was sending such messages, she didn't hesitate.

"I want to meet you in person," she said.

"No," I replied, firmly.

Then came another request: "At least on a video call? I want to see you and talk to you."

"Why?" I asked, confused, unsettled.

Her reply came almost instantly.

"I had a female friend once," she wrote. "We used to meet on weekends, in private, and spend personal time together. When I saw your painted lips that day... I don't know. I felt intoxicated. I want to meet you. It's safe. Nothing to worry. There's no harm in meeting and talking. But society is cruel. They label us... they call us lesbians. And we have to carry that blame."

Her words stunned me. The thought froze me.

I stared at the screen, my thoughts racing. There was no judgment in my heart—only surprise, and a sudden realization of how different our lives were. What she was expressing, I couldn't relate to. Not because I was angry, not because I looked down on her, but because I simply didn't feel the same way.

After that, I said nothing.

Days passed. Then a week. The messages stopped. The silence returned.

That was her world—a world of longing, of hidden spaces and unspoken desires. I had mine—calmer, quieter, more solitary, with its own set of rules and dreams.

We were two women—two ladies—each walking her own path. Different perspectives. Different lives.

22
Unnis Birthday

It was Unni's birthday. The house was buzzing with children—laughing, playing, shouting with joy. The floor was scattered with balloons and wrappers, and the table was piled high with colourful gifts.

Among the kids was one older boy—taller than the rest, quieter too. He stood a little apart, his eyes fixed on the presents Unni was opening, one after another. He didn't speak, didn't smile. He just watched.

Unni's aunt leaned down and whispered to her son, "My kid, keep all your toys safe. That boy will play with them and spoil them. He's never had a toy in his life. How could he? There isn't even food in his house."

Unni's mother added softly, "Take your toys and hide them somewhere he can't see."

Just then, the front door opened. A man walked in, holding a big toy wrapped in shiny gift paper. There was a faint smell of sweat clinging to him, and his shirt was creased with the marks of a long day.

"I was busy with some work. That's why I'm late," he said to Unni's father, wiping his forehead. He looked tired—exhausted, even.

Still, his face lit up as he turned to Unni. With eyes full of joy and a heart overflowing with prayers, he handed the gift to the birthday boy and wished him warmly.

The room fell quiet for a moment—not because of the gift, but because of the way the older boy's eyes sparkled as he looked at it. They were wide, full of something no one could name. Hope, maybe. Or longing. Or just the pure joy of seeing something beautiful up close.

Would he be allowed to play with this toy, even for a little while?

After all, it was a gift from his father—to Unni.